The Knights
of Can-a-Lot

One morning, someone arrived at Bob's yard. His name was Bob, too. "Hi, Dad," said Bob. "I didn't expect you until the summer."

"I was bored at home," explained Bob's dad. "I need a project to do."

Then the telephone rang and Bob's dad answered.
"Hello, this is Dr Mountfitchett. Castle Camelot
needs fixing.
Can you help?"

Dr Mountfitchett came to Bob's yard and showed Bob's dad a plan of the castle. She thought he was Bob the builder!

"We'll go over to Castle Camelot now to take a look," Bob's dad said.

There was a moat around the castle, so they couldn't reach it to go inside.
"Knights – like Sir Lancelot – would lower a drawbridge over the moat to let in friends, and raise it to keep out enemies," explained Dr Mountfitchett.

"That's your first job, team," said Bob's dad. "Build a drawbridge."

"Can we build Camelot?" called Scoop.

"Yes, we can!" giggled Dizzy. "Camelot…Can-a-lot. We can a lot!"

"Meet the knights of Can-a-lot!" laughed Muck. "Bob's dad is Sir Boss-a-lot!"

Bob's dad decided
to mend the castle gate.
But then…
"Help!" he yelled. "I'm stuck!"
Bob's dad was stuck to
the chains that raised and
lowered the gate. Lofty
had to rescue him with
his hook.

To keep his dad out of trouble, Bob persuaded him to clip the maze hedges. Then...

"Help," shouted Bob's dad. "I'm lost in the maze!"

Lofty had to lift Bob high up so that he could see his dad and tell him how to get out.

Bob was clipping
some ivy when he found
a hidden door.

"It's the lost door
to the dungeon!" cried
Dr Mountfitchett.
Bob and his dad pushed it
open and the three of them went inside.
But Bob's dad closed the door by mistake.
They were trapped!

Bob's dad bravely went off to look for a way out. He fell against a wall, and it opened. He was pushed out in the maze again!

Bob's dad cut through the hedges to escape
from the maze!

"Oh no!" said Bob when he saw the hedges.
"They're ruined!"

Dr Mountfitchett thought the hedges looked wonderful.
"They're shaped like knights," she beamed.

When the castle
was fixed, there was
a grand opening
with lots of visitors, including
Bob's mum. Everyone had
dressed up.
"Who's going to be king?"
asked Dr Mountfitchett.
"You can be King Dad," said Bob.
"No, you'd make a better king," insisted Bob's dad.

So Bob declared, "I, King of Can-a-lot, knight thee. Arise, Sir Dad-a-lot!"

THE END!